The Nightlife of Jacuzzi Gaskett

The Nightlife of Jacuzzi Gaskett

WRITTEN BY
Brontez Purnell

ILLUSTRATED BY
Elise R. Peterson

dottir press
NEW YORK CITY

Published in 2019 by Dottir Press
33 Fifth Avenue
New York, NY 10003

Dottirpress.com

Trade distribution through Consortium Book Sales and Distribution, www.cbsd.com.

Special discounts are available for bulk purchases by organizations and institutions.
Please contact jb@dottirpress.com to inquire.

FIRST EDITION

First printing: January 2019
Production and design by Drew Stevens
Photos on page 48 © Beowulf Sheehan (Brontez Purnell) and © Hans Neuman (Elise R. Peterson)

Library of Congress Cataloging-in-Publication Data is available for this title.
ISBN 978-1-9483-4002-1

Manufactured by Thomson-Shore, Dexter, MI (USA); RMA258KN78, October 2018

This book is dedicated to my mother, Annie Jewel, who taught me the importance of writing and fearlessness, my sister Danielle who loved and protected me, and the absolute loves of my life, my nephews Ethan and Cooper, who taught me that my work as an older brother is never, ever done. —BP

To my mother, Lisa, who selflessly showed me love, and to my son, Sargent, who taught me how to do the same.—ERP

His name was John Gaskett Clements.

He went by "Gaskett" at school, though. There were thirteen other Johns in his class. He went by his middle name so people would be sure to remember him.

His nickname was "Jacuzzi,"

because that was where he was conceived.

Jacuzzi had just turned 11.

His house was a good five-minute walk from the spot where the school bus dropped him off every day. In another thirty minutes his mother would be home to drop off his baby brother Jamaal from the babysitter's.

His brother was 11 months old.

His brother was his new favorite person.

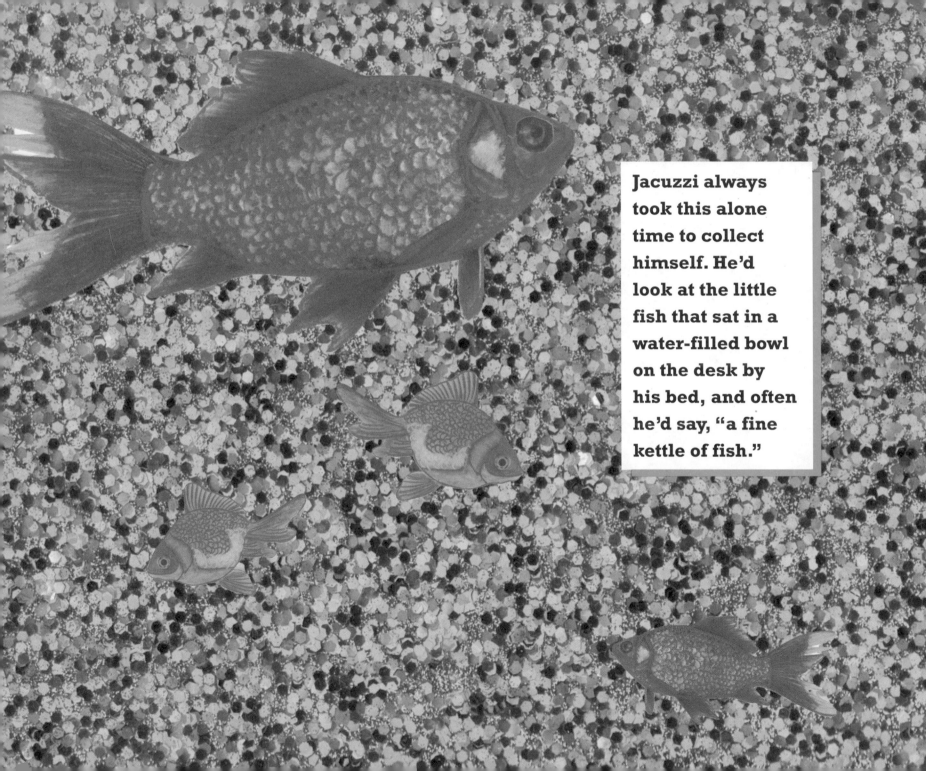

Jacuzzi always took this alone time to collect himself. He'd look at the little fish that sat in a water-filled bowl on the desk by his bed, and often he'd say, "a fine kettle of fish."

He didn't know why he said "a fine kettle of fish"—other than the fact that his grandfather had come in his room once, a long time ago, peered into his fish bowl, and said, "Ah, a fine kettle of fish." (The fish from this memory were already dead.)

Jacuzzi went into the kitchen and stared at the stove. "Better not play with fire again," he reminded himself.

He went to his room and looked at the cardboard box filled with multi-colored Legos. He was tired of building the same things: trains, airplanes, and spaceships. Instead, he took the box and heaved the entire contents into the air. The Legos hit the ceiling and hurtled right back to earth.

Jacuzzi considered the dense collection of multicolored plastic at his feet and decided it was a strange art installation, meant to be displayed on the floor.

Then he heard brisk footsteps on the cement stairs attached to his second-story apartment. "Mama and Jamaal are home," he said, but just in his head. Mama worked with soldiers at the army base and she carried the same percussion in her step, her knock, and her general way.

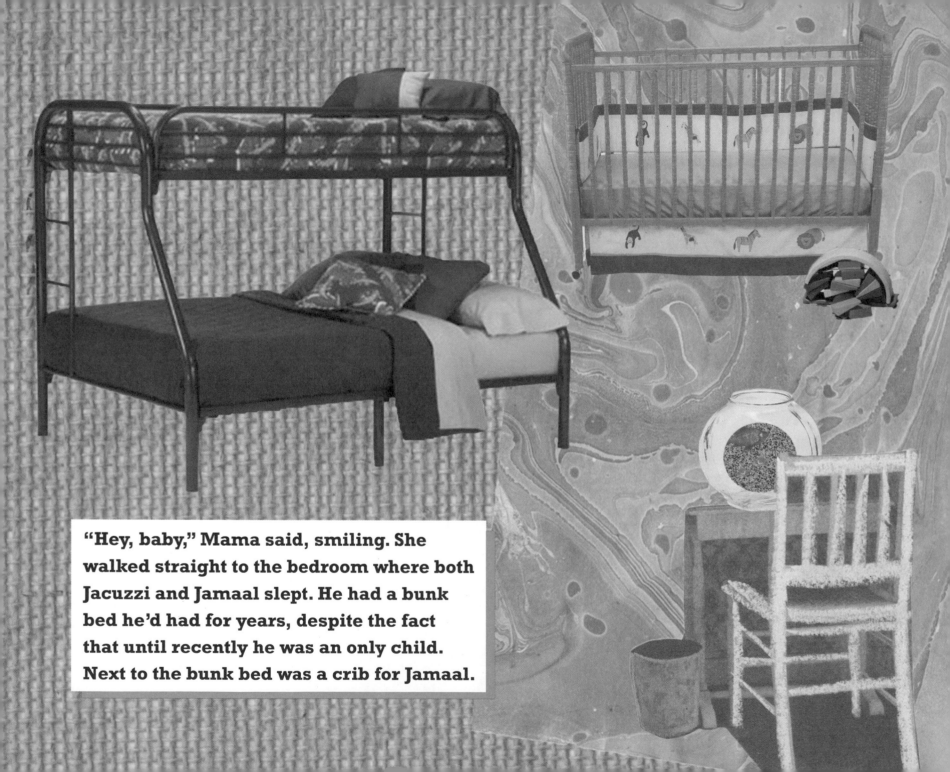

"Hey, baby," Mama said, smiling. She walked straight to the bedroom where both Jacuzzi and Jamaal slept. He had a bunk bed he'd had for years, despite the fact that until recently he was an only child. Next to the bunk bed was a crib for Jamaal.

"Mama has to hurry, baby," she said, zipping by to put Jamaal down in his crib and change out of her work clothes. She always had the same routine. She tidied up the apartment here and there, gave Jamaal a bath, and prepared bottles for him. Then she heated up food for Jacuzzi, kissed him on the forehead, and asked about his day. "Mama's leaving in a bit—I'm going to feed Jamaal, then you have to look after him," she said. "You are Mama's big boy."

Mama was going to her boyfriend's house. Jacuzzi hated him. That summer, the boyfriend had insisted that Mama sign him up for basketball, but Jacuzzi hated basketball. And football. And baseball. And (maybe most of all) soccer. "It's just a bunch of people running and yelling," he explained one time to the boyfriend, who gave Jacuzzi a very disappointed look.

Jacuzzi watched his mom move through her pre-going-out ritual. She (for a good two months now) would shower (or just spray on deodorant), put on makeup, do her hair, and kiss Jacuzzi goodbye. She was always home by 2 a.m.

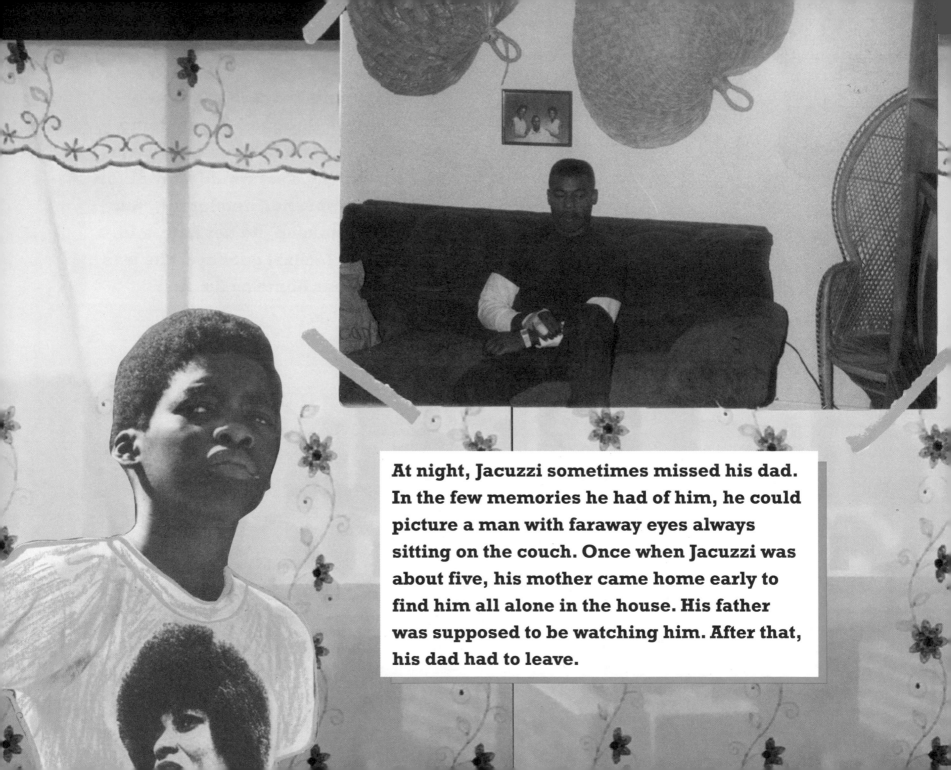

At night, Jacuzzi sometimes missed his dad. In the few memories he had of him, he could picture a man with faraway eyes always sitting on the couch. Once when Jacuzzi was about five, his mother came home early to find him all alone in the house. His father was supposed to be watching him. After that, his dad had to leave.

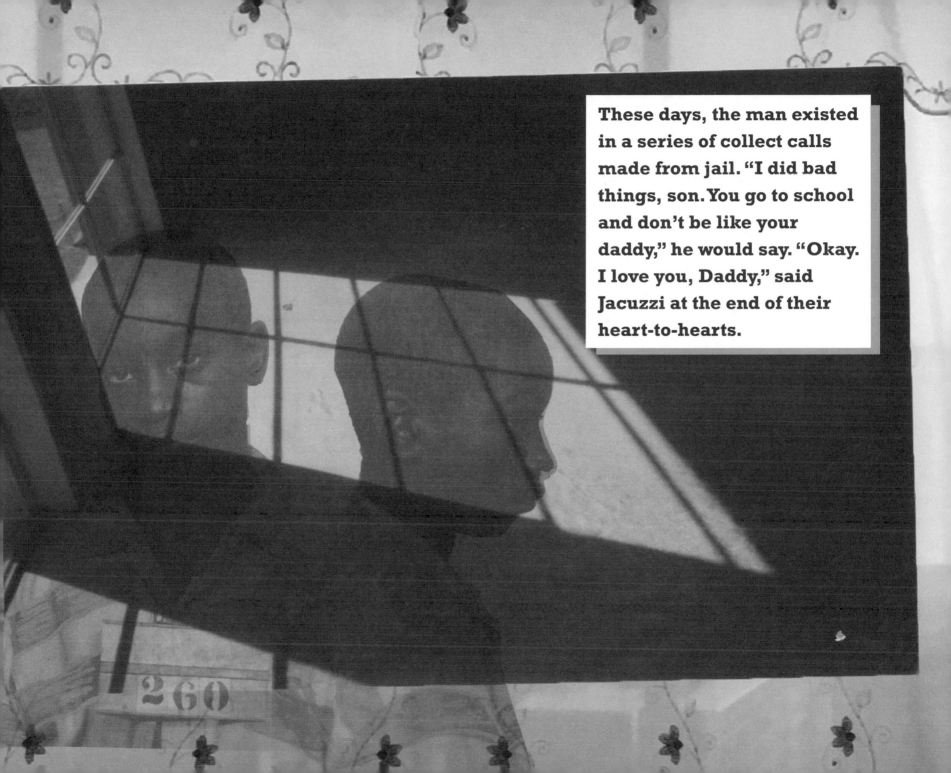

These days, the man existed in a series of collect calls made from jail. "I did bad things, son. You go to school and don't be like your daddy," he would say. "Okay. I love you, Daddy," said Jacuzzi at the end of their heart-to-hearts.

Oh! Now he heard his baby brother crying. He retrieved wailing Jamaal from his crib and sat on the couch to rock him in his arms back and forth like his mom had taught him. Like *magic*, the infant was quiet the instant the rocking started.

Jacuzzi looked at lil' Jamaal. He smelled him. (He liked the way babies smelled.) "You're my only friend," he whispered to the baby's little head.

Jacuzzi let his mind wander to the rest of his life.

The truth was he hated school and all the people in it. They all made fun of him. No one seemed to see how smart or special he was.

Earlier that day, the students in his class had to present a paper on what their future career would be. Emily Dougansmif wrote a paper about how she wanted to be a doctor and got an A+. Mike Tollins presented a paper about how he wanted to be a garbage man like his dad and got a C.

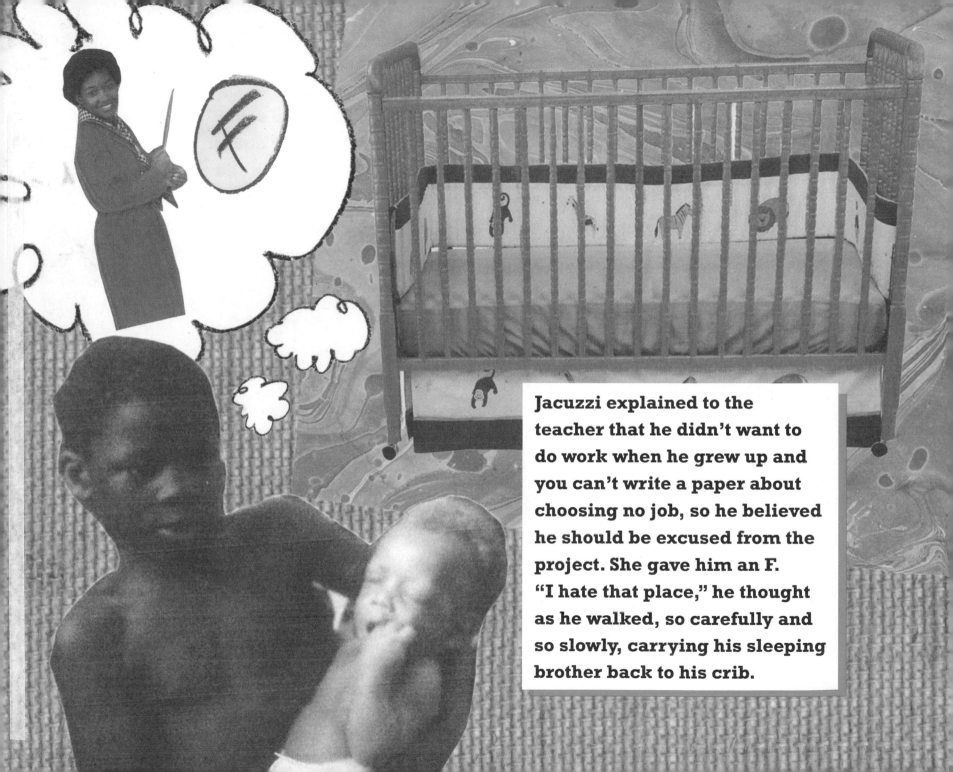

Jacuzzi explained to the teacher that he didn't want to do work when he grew up and you can't write a paper about choosing no job, so he believed he should be excused from the project. She gave him an F. "I hate that place," he thought as he walked, so carefully and so slowly, carrying his sleeping brother back to his crib.

The month before, Jacuzzi didn't go on the school field trip to the Jelly Bean Factory because his mom couldn't afford it, so he had to stay in the library all day. He tended to stay in the library anyway, whenever he could. He liked the books.

In one book, he read about how there were crystal skulls in Mexico, and in another he read about how the ghost of some woman haunted a beach in Hawaii. He wanted to get to those places. In another book, he learned that the next neighboring galaxy was called Andromeda. He *really* wanted to get there.

Skulls, ghosts, and stars were interesting, but mythology was the most interesting.

Jacuzzi had taken out a library book about a god in Africa that controlled the wind and rain and this sparked an idea in his head.

He filled the blender with water and carried it into the living room as carefully as he carried Jamaal. He placed the lid on top and pressed the "purée" button. A contained little cyclone whirred *go go go* inside the glass. He added green food coloring to the water for effect. "I can make tornadoes!" he said.

"I'm a *god*," Jacuzzi said to no one in particular as he put away the blender, which was heavy.

Next order of business was that there was no next order of business, so Jacuzzi decided to go to bed.

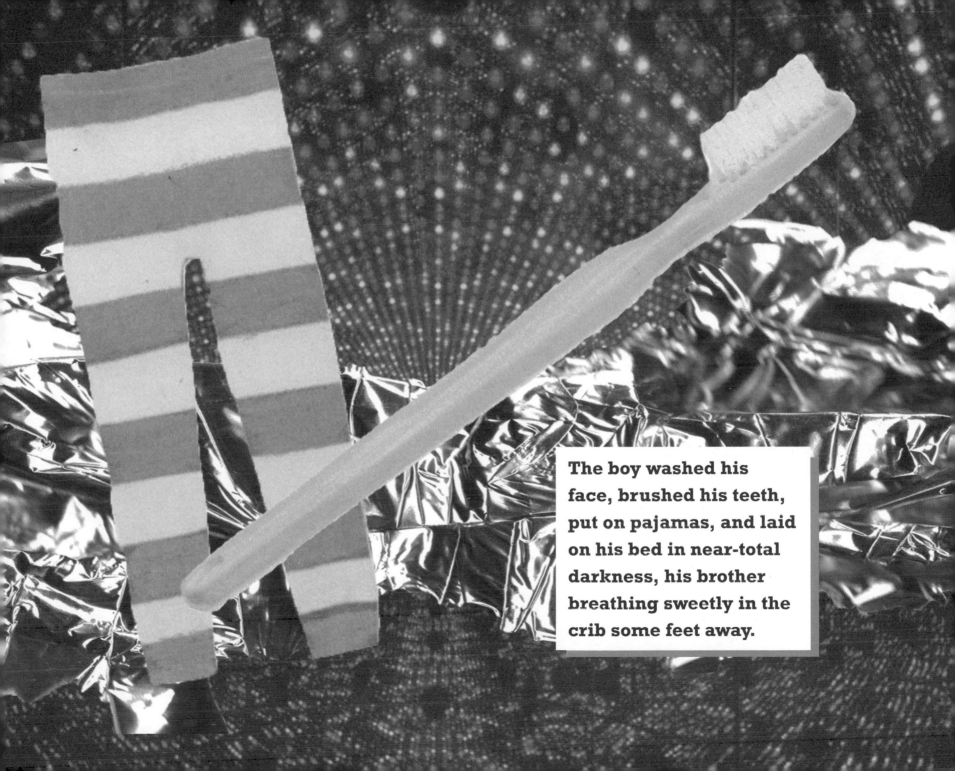

The boy washed his face, brushed his teeth, put on pajamas, and laid on his bed in near-total darkness, his brother breathing sweetly in the crib some feet away.

Above him, a galaxy of mini stars glowed when you turned off the light. On nights like tonight, Jacuzzi would count the stars until he dozed off, then he'd wake up and do it again.

He would continue this pattern until his mom came home. Sometimes he would get to six full countings, other times to seven.

This particular night he couldn't stop thinking about the Andromeda galaxy.

He wondered about all the people there and what they were doing.

He wondered if the boys in the Andromeda galaxy had dads, or teachers who didn't pick on them, or baby brothers they had to take care of. He felt a little sad at the idea of all those people so far away having fun without him.

"I really, truly have to get there," Jacuzzi vowed as he began his seventh round of counting. Just then, he heard keys opening the front door.

Mama was home.

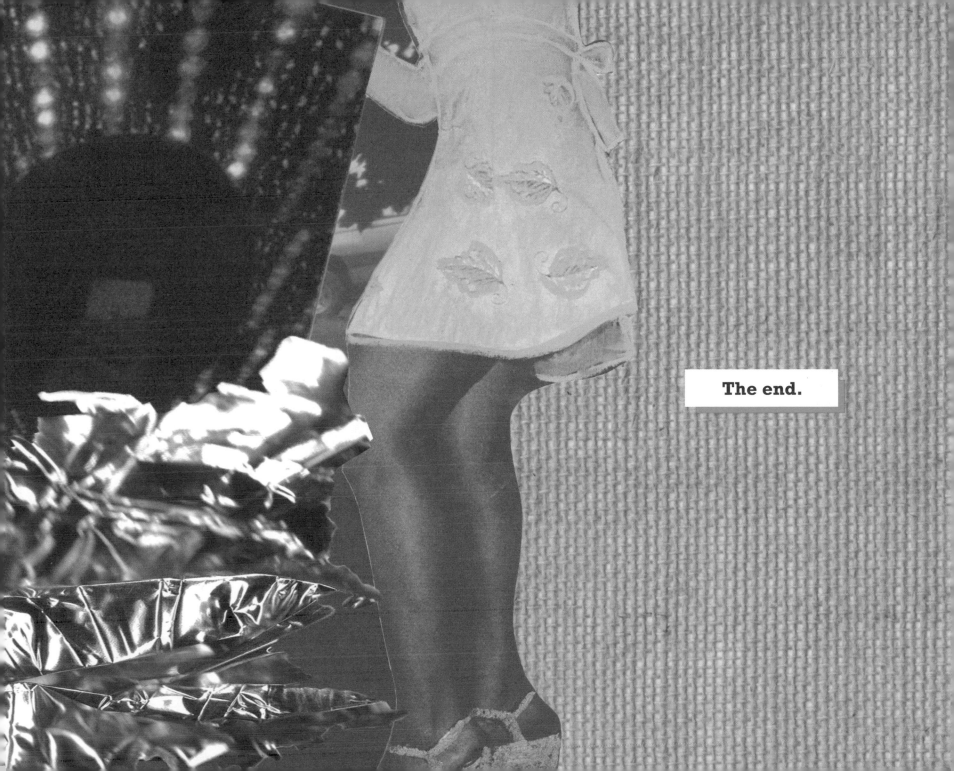

The end.

Brontez Purnell is a zine-maker, punk drummer, choreographer, and winner of a Whiting Award for his 2017 novella *Since I Laid My Burden Down*. Originally from Alabama, he lives in Oakland, California.

Elise R. Peterson is an artist and writer living in Brooklyn. She illustrated the children's book *How Mamas Love Their Babies*.